Karen's Cooking
Contest

**Other books by
Ann M. Martin**

Leo the Magnificat
Rachel Parker, Kindergarten Show-off
Eleven Kids, One Summer
Ma and Pa Dracula
Yours Turly, Shirley
Ten Kids, No Pets
With You and Without You
Me and Katie (the Pest)
Stage Fright
Inside Out
Bummer Summer

For older readers:

Missing Since Monday
Just a Summer Romance
Slam Book

THE BABY-SITTERS CLUB series
THE BABY-SITTERS CLUB mysteries
THE KIDS IN MS. COLMAN'S CLASS series
BABY-SITTERS LITTLE SISTER series
(see inside book covers for a complete listing)

Little Sister

Karen's Cooking Contest

Ann M. Martin

Illustrations by Susan Tang

A
LITTLE APPLE
PAPERBACK

SCHOLASTIC INC.
New York Toronto London Auckland Sydney

The author gratefully acknowledges
Gabrielle Charbonnet
for her help
with this book.

ISBN 0-590-06591-2

12 11 10 9 8 7 6 5 4 3 2   8 9/9 0 1/0 2/0

Printed in the U.S.A.   40
First Scholastic printing, January 1998

Back at School

"Who is Mark Fitzpatrick?" asked Pamela Harding.

"He is the weatherman for Channel Seven," said Nancy Dawes.

Pamela snorted. "A weatherman is not a real celebrity," she said.

"Is too," said Nancy.

"Is not," said Pamela.

That is when I stopped listening. I knew Nancy could stand up for herself against Pamela. After all, she has had a lot of prac-

tice. We all have. That is because Pamela is the class meanie-mo.

We are in Ms. Colman's second-grade class at Stoneybrook Academy, in Stoneybrook, Connecticut. Nancy and Pamela were disagreeing about our latest class project. Of course, I was on Nancy's side. Mark Fitzpatrick counts as a celebrity. He is on television, after all.

You might be wondering who I am. I will give you some clues:

1) I am not the class meanie-mo.
2) I am seven years old.
3) Nancy Dawes and Hannie Papadakis are my two best friends. Together, we are the Three Musketeers.

Give up? I am Karen Brewer! You will find out a lot more about me soon.

Our class project was going to be gigundoly fun. Before our winter vacation, Ms. Colman (who is the best teacher in the whole wide world) had asked us each to write letters to five celebrities. We asked the celebrities to write back and send us their favorite recipes. When all our celebrities' recipes are here, we will type them neatly on our class computer and make them into a real cookbook.

It will be a very special and glamorous cookbook.

Nancy had chosen a local weatherman as one of her celebrities. Pamela had chosen only huge superstars. I bet Nancy would hear from her celebrities before Pamela heard from hers.

I had chosen really fun people: my favorite author, my favorite movie star, my favorite singer, the owner of Funland, and finally, my favorite gymnast. I could not wait for them to write back and send me their favorite recipes. Though sometimes I wondered whether they would even *have* favorite recipes. Maybe because they are rich and famous, they just eat out all the time. Or maybe they have chefs at home and never cook for themselves. If their chef sent in a

4

recipe, would it count? I hoped so.

"Remember, class," said Ms. Colman. "If you do not hear from your celebrities, you may ask a family member for a recipe instead."

"A family member!" said Pamela. "That would be almost as boring as Nancy's weatherman."

"Mark Fitzpatrick is a celebrity!" cried Nancy.

Ms. Colman held up her hand. "That will be enough of that," she said.

"Hmphh. No one wants to use a family member," muttered Pamela.

For once, I had to agree with Pamela (though I did not say so out loud). Using a recipe from a family member would not be nearly as special or glamorous as a recipe from a celebrity. After all, a celebrity's recipe would probably be for Oysters Rockefeller or something. A family recipe would be for meat loaf.

I really hoped I would not have to ask for a family member's recipe. For one thing, it would mean choosing between my two families. In my big-house family, Nannie does most of the cooking. At the little house, Mommy and Seth do the cooking. I love all of them. It would not be easy to choose which one to ask for a recipe. Hmm. I guess I should explain my two houses and my two families.

Home Cooking

This month is a big-house month. That means I live with Daddy and my big-house family. Next month, February, will be a little-house month. I will live with Mommy and my little-house family.

A long time ago, every month was a big-house month. Back then, I only had one family: me, Mommy, Daddy, and my little brother, Andrew. (He is four going on five.) Then Mommy and Daddy got divorced. So Andrew and I went to live with Mommy in the little house. (Daddy stayed at the big house. It is the house he grew up in.) After awhile, Mommy got married again, to Seth Engle. He is my stepfather. (He is very, very nice. He makes beautiful furniture out of wood.) So now my little-house family is Mommy, Seth, Andrew, Rocky (Seth's dog), Midgie (Seth's cat), Emily Junior (my rat), and Bob (Andrew's hermit crab).

Back at the big house, Daddy got married again too, to Elizabeth Thomas. She already had four children. Sam and Charlie are teenagers. They go to Stoneybrook High School. Kristy is thirteen. She is a terrific big sister. David Michael is seven years old, but he doesn't go to my school. He goes to Stoneybrook Elementary.

Daddy and Elizabeth adopted my little sister, Emily Michelle, from a country called Vietnam. She is two and a half years old. And Elizabeth's mother, Nannie, came to live at the big house to help take care of all the people and the pets. Shannon is David Michael's big puppy. Boo-Boo is Daddy's grumpy old cat. Andrew and I have two

8

goldfish. Their names are Goldfishie and Crystal Light the Second. And Emily Junior and Bob live at the big house whenever Andrew and I do. So you can see that the big house is pretty full!

Andrew and I live at the little house one month, and at the big house one month. We go back and forth between our two houses, which is one of the reasons I call us Andrew Two-Two and Karen Two-Two. Besides families and houses, I have two of lots of things: stuffed cats, bicycles, beds. Not only that, but I even wear two pairs of glasses — the blue ones are for reading up close, and the pink ones are for the rest of the time. And I already told you about my two best friends, Hannie and Nancy.

That afternoon, when I got home from school, Nannie was fixing dinner. It smelled delicious. I could hardly wait until it was time to eat.

There are so many of us at the big house that we sit at a very long kitchen table, on two very long benches. Tonight I was sitting between Andrew and Elizabeth. (I usually try to sit next to Kristy.)

"Ahem," I said, once everyone had been served. (We were having vegetable lasagna. Yum!) "I would like to tell you about my class project."

"Go ahead, honey," said Elizabeth.

I told my big-house family about our celebrity-recipe cookbook, and how I hoped all five of my celebrities would write back soon.

"Do not get your hopes up," said Sam. "Celebrities hardly ever answer their fan mail."

"Do not discourage her," said Kristy. "I think it is a neat idea. And I bet all of your celebrities will come through for you, Karen."

"Thank you," I said. (Kristy is so nice.)

"Let me know if you need a family member's recipe," said David Michael. "I have one for worm cake that I could give you."

I gave David Michael a Look. Sam and Charlie laughed.

"I think your project sounds lovely, Karen," Elizabeth said. "What will your class do with these cookbooks once they are finished?"

"We are going to sell them in the school library," I said. "We will give the money to the library so they can buy more books."

"That is great, Karen," said Daddy.

"I have an announcement too," said Nannie. "I am going to enter a cooking contest. It is being sponsored by the Cocoa-Best chocolate company. They will award a prize for the best recipe using their chocolate."

"Yum, chocolate! That sounds like fun," I said.

"Does anyone want to help me with the contest?" asked Nannie.

"No, thanks. Count me out," said Sam.

"I am pretty busy right now," said Kristy.

"I will help you!" I cried. "I am very good at contests."

"Thank you, Karen," said Nannie. "We will get started this weekend."

"Now I have an announcement," said Daddy. "You all know the little butler's pantry by the mudroom?"

We nodded. The big house really is big. In fact, it is a mansion. There are three floors and nine bedrooms. The kitchen is huge (but cozy). I had practically forgotten about the little pantry by the mudroom. Nannie uses the bigger, modern pantry attached to the kitchen.

"It is just sitting there going to waste," said Daddy. "It is full of junk no one uses. Not only that, but the walls are crumbling, and the window leaks when it rains."

"What should we do about it?" asked Elizabeth.

"That is what I wanted to ask all of you," said Daddy. "We should fix it up and turn it into a useful room. But I cannot think of what to do with it. So I want each of you to come up with ideas. We can discuss them as a family and decide what we should turn the pantry into."

Oh, boy! I thought. This could be fun.

Chocolate Magic

"Chocolate fudge?" I asked.

Nannie thought for a moment. "No," she said.

I flipped through the cookbook pages again. It was Saturday morning. Nannie and I were starting to work on her chocolate recipe for the contest.

"Chocolate-chip cookies?" I said. "You make great chocolate-chip cookies."

"Too ordinary," said Nannie. "Everyone and his brother will be baking cookies."

I looked in the cookbook again.

Nannie flipped through the pages of another cookbook. "Brownies?" she asked me.

"I do not know," I said. "I think a lot of people will be making brownies too."

"Chocolate mousse?" asked Nannie.

"What is that?" I said.

"Like chocolate pudding."

"Well, maybe chocolate pudding, even fancy chocolate pudding, is not really different enough."

"Here is one," said Nannie. "It is for a dipping chocolate. It is a chocolate sauce. You dip strawberries or other fruit in it and it hardens like chocolate candy. Or you can pour it over ice cream. A recipe for dipping chocolate is pretty unusual."

"It sounds great," I said. "Especially poured over ice cream."

"Let me make a list of the ingredients I need," said Nannie.

Nannie experimented with the recipe for a long time. The contest recipe had to be original, so Nannie could not just use the one from the cookbook. It had to be her own special recipe. She added some vanilla, and she used less sugar. We had to do many taste tests.

"This one tastes great," said Nannie. "But when you dip fruit in it, the chocolate does not get hard."

"It has to get hard," I agreed. "Or it will be too messy to eat."

"Also, you could not set the fruit in a box or on a platter," said Nannie. "I will have to fix it."

I helped Nannie all weekend. We had bought pounds and pounds of Cocoa-Best chocolate. We melted it and mixed it and added this and that. My job was to wash the strawberries and other fruit for the dipping. We tried bananas, oranges, strawberries, and even raisins and peanuts.

You will not believe this, but I almost got tired of chocolate. We tried the chocolate sauce on ice cream and on cake, and tried dipping cookies in it too.

"This looks great," said Charlie, popping a cookie in his mouth.

We waited.

Charlie chewed the cookie and swallowed it. "It is good, but maybe just a little too sweet," he said. "Could you make it less sweet?"

Nannie and I sighed. Back to the drawing board.

"Mmmm," said Kristy. "This is really good. I think the strawberries and the pretzels are the best."

"I think so too," said Nannie. She smiled at me, and I gave her a thumbs-up. (If you have never eaten a chocolate-covered pretzel, you might think it sounds yucky. But it is yummy.)

"What do you say, Karen?" asked Nannie. "Is this the one?"

I nodded. "I think so, Nannie. It is sweet, but not too sweet. It is a nice chocolatey color. It gets hard after you dip something in

it. It is good and shiny. I think it may be perfect."

"Okay, then," said Nannie. "I will write down exactly what we used and how we made it. We will not tell anyone else what is in it. It will be our super-secret recipe. And we might just win the contest!"

Recipes, Recipes

"I got one!" cried Chris Lamar. "I got one!"

It was Wednesday morning. Chris had just picked up the mail for Ms. Colman's class. Recipes from celebrities had started arriving at our school office. Jannie Gilbert had received one. So had Hank Reubens, Addie Sidney, Sara Ford, Leslie Morris, Pamela Harding (boo and bullfrogs), and Omar Harris. Ricky Torres, my pretend husband, had received two. So had Hannie and Bobby Gianelli. The rest of us — me, Tammy

19

and Terri Barkan (they are twins), Ian Johnson, Audrey Green, Nancy, and Natalie Springer — had not heard from our celebrities yet.

Every day I looked through Ms. Colman's stack of mail. Every day there was nothing for me.

Chris ripped open his envelope. Inside was a signed picture of Tough Tommy Blackcat. (Lots of the other celebrities had sent signed pictures also.) "Look!" said Chris, holding up the picture. "It shows Tough Tommy on his motorcycle. He looks like he is about to go fight the bad guys." Chris waved the picture around.

"What is his recipe?" asked Bobby.

Chris looked in the envelope again. He pulled out a piece of paper. "It is for bean dip."

"Ew, gross," said Bobby, wrinkling his nose.

"I like bean dip," said Chris. "It is good with tortilla chips."

"Beans, beans, they're good for your

heart," sang Bobby. "The more you eat, the more you —"

"Okay, Bobby," said Ms. Colman. "We get the picture. Chris, would you please put your recipe in our recipe file?"

"How many recipes do we have now?" asked Addie. She rolled her wheelchair closer to the computer table.

Chris counted them. "Fourteen."

"That is not enough for a cookbook," said Addie. "We will need many more than that."

"I am sure we will hear from more celebrities," said Ms. Colman. "But just to be on the safe side, maybe we should ask family members for recipes also."

"Nooo," said Pamela. "It should be a celebrity-only cookbook."

"We will try to make it a celebrity-only cookbook," said Ms. Colman. "But if that does not work we may fill it in with family recipes. They could be very interesting. Some family recipes have been passed down for generations. You might have one that is for special occasions, or for holidays. In the cookbook we could explain about the recipe. People would like to read about them."

"I guess," said Pamela.

Addie had been looking through the recipes. "We may have another problem," she said. She had spread the recipes out on her wheelchair tray. "Some of these recipes sound okay. But some sound kind of weird. There is a Jell-O recipe here that uses Coca-Cola. That does not sound very healthy."

"That sounds disgusting," I said.

"We will have to go through the recipes and decide which ones to include in our cookbook," said Ms. Colman. "We may have to leave some of them out. Which is why it would be good to have as many recipes as possible. So do think about asking your family members to contribute."

Hmm, I thought. So far I had not heard from any of my celebrities. But I was certain I would. I just had to. I did not want to use a family member's recipe. What would I turn in? David Michael's worm cake?

Round One

On Saturday afternoon I got to do something very special. It was the first day of the chocolate-recipe contest. Nannie and I took her dipping chocolate to a hotel in downtown Stoneybrook. That was where the first round of the judging would take place.

At the hotel, a sign in the lobby said COCOA-BEST CHOCOLATE COOK-OFF, THIS WAY. We followed the sign to the large ballroom in the hotel. Inside were many rows of tables covered with white cloths.

Nannie gave her name to a lady at a table

by the door and paid her entrance fee. Then together we found a table with a sign that said JANET TAYLOR. (That is Nannie's real name.)

I helped Nannie get ready. First I put up another sign that I had made myself. It said CHOCOLATE MAGIC on it. That was what Nannie had decided to call her dipping chocolate. I had used brown markers and gold glitter on the sign. It looked much fancier than any of the other signs I saw.

On our table Nannie set a serving dish on a little stand. In the stand was a small candle. The candle would keep the chocolate warm during the contest. (Dipping chocolate is liquid when it is warm, and hard when it is cool.)

Nannie took out a cookie sheet and covered it with waxed paper. Then, while she was filling in some papers for the contest, I started dipping.

First I took a long wooden toothpick and stuck it into a strawberry. Then I dipped almost the whole strawberry in the warm

chocolate. I swirled it carefully, just the way Nannie had shown me. When the strawberry was covered with a thick layer of chocolate, I placed it gently on the cookie sheet. Ta-daaa!

"That looks perfect, Karen," said Nannie. She finished her paperwork and started dipping with me.

All around us people were setting up their tables. There were lots of women and lots of men. And there was chocolate everything: cakes, cookies, brownies, sauces, candies in fancy shapes, chocolate decorations, chocolate drinks . . . and there were two other people who were fixing chocolate-dipped fruit.

The judges were two men and one woman from the Cocoa-Best company. They gave a little speech, and then started walking around the room tasting everything.

"I am so nervous," whispered Nannie.

"Do not be nervous," I whispered back. "Your Chocolate Magic will definitely win. It is the best. And you know what? There are twelve people here with chocolate-chip cookies. There are only three dipping chocolates."

"I am glad we did not make cookies," said Nannie.

It was very, very hard to wait for our turn. I always have trouble waiting for anything. But I tried to be patient.

Finally the judges came to our table. I pushed the Chocolate Magic sign a little closer to them. The judges peered at our samples on the cookie sheet.

"Nice color," murmured one judge.

"Good sheen," said another.

"Very rich-looking," said the third.

I turned to Nannie and wiggled my eyebrows. She smiled at me.

Then the judges started tasting. They each tried a strawberry, a pretzel, and a tiny chocolate-covered cake. Then they each took another piece of chocolate-dipped fruit.

In between the samples, they sipped water and made notes in their notebooks. I could hardly stand the excitement. I crossed the fingers of both hands behind my back, and tried to cross my toes inside my sneakers.

"Thank you very much," said one judge. "We will now confer, and decide on our winners."

I could not sit still while the judges huddled at the front of the ballroom, whispering to each other. I felt as if I would have to jump up and start running around. But I did not. I sampled other people's recipes. (We were allowed to do this. Everyone was doing it. It is a good thing we had brought lots of samples of Chocolate Magic.)

I tasted many delicious chocolate things, but nothing was as good as Nannie's Chocolate Magic. And I am not just saying that.

Finally the judges called for our attention. "We have a winner," one man announced. "The first-place blue ribbon goes to . . . Janet Taylor, for her Chocolate Magic!"

"Oh, my goodness!" cried Nannie. She and I stared at each other. Then I leaped into her arms.

"Congratulations, Nannie!" I yelled. "Hooray!"

We began jumping up and down. The judges came to Nannie's table and pinned a huge blue ribbon to the cloth.

"Congratulations, Mrs. Taylor," each of the judges said. All three of them shook Nannie's hand. Then they shook my hand too. I felt very proud and important. After all, I had done a lot of the dipping and swirling. Not to mention a lot of the taste-testing.

"The first-place prize in this, the first round of the Cocoa-Best Chocolate Cook-off, is a fifty-dollar gift certificate," said the lady judge. "It is good for any of the many Cocoa-Best products wherever they are sold."

"Thank you very much," said Nannie. She took the certificate and smiled. Someone from the *Stoneybrook News* took a picture of Nannie and me each holding one side of the certificate. I smiled extra big.

"And of course we will see you next week

in Hartford," said the second judge. "For round two of the cook-off."

"Round two?" I asked.

"Today's contest was just for Stoneybrook," explained Nannie. "Next week's contest is for all of Connecticut. Then comes all of the states in the Northeast."

"Wow," I said. "We better get to work!"

Tasty Treats

"How many recipes do we have so far?" asked Terri Barkan on Tuesday morning. The bell had not rung yet, but most of us were already in Ms. Colman's room.

Addie Sidney counted. "Forty-five," she said.

"Forty-five!" I exclaimed. "We have heard from forty-five celebrities?" (None of them was mine.)

Addie shook her head. "No. Some celebrities sent more than one recipe."

"I have heard from all five of my celebrities," said Pamela. She tossed her long hair over one shoulder. I gritted my teeth.

Pamela turned to Nancy. "Did you ever hear from your weatherman?"

"Yes," said Nancy. "For your information, I did. And he sent a pot roast recipe that sounds delicious."

Pamela tossed her hair again and went to the back of the room to talk to her two best friends, Jannie Gilbert and Leslie Morris.

I sat down at my desk and put my head in my hands.

Nancy guessed what was wrong. "Do not worry, Karen," she said. "I am sure you will hear from a celebrity soon."

"It has been a *long* time," I said.

"Yes, but some people are just taking longer," said Nancy.

"Nancy is right," said Hannie. "I have received only two replies. Nancy has gotten three. A bunch of kids have heard from just one person. And you are not the only one who has not gotten any letters yet."

I made a face. "Only me, Audrey, and

Natalie. We are losers in the cookbook project."

"Karen, I do not like to hear that," said Ms. Colman from her desk. (I sit in the very front row, because I am a glasses-wearer. The other glasses-wearers are Ricky and Natalie and Ms. Colman. My desk is right in front of Ms. Colman's desk.)

"I do not think anyone in my class is a loser," said Ms. Colman. "If you have not received a letter yet, you may participate in other ways. For example, it is time for us to think of a title for our cookbook. As soon as class begins, I will collect suggestions. And we will also need some art. In the meantime, you may still hear from your celebrities. Okay?"

"Okay," I said. Ms. Colman always knows how to make me feel better.

That morning we wrote down our cookbook title suggestions on a piece of paper.

"Ms. Colman!" I said. "I have many excellent suggestions for a title. Should I write them all down?"

"No, Karen," said Ms. Colman. "Just choose your favorite."

Boo and bullfrogs. In the end, I chose *Give Your Mouth a Party.*

Next Ms. Colman split our class into three groups of six kids. Each group had to choose just one person's title. My group did not choose *Give Your Mouth a Party.* Instead, they voted for Nancy's title, which was *Tasty Treats.*

I decided that if they did not want to use my title, then I was happy that they wanted to use Nancy's. After each group had picked a title, the class voted on the three titles. You know what? Nancy's title won again!

"*Tasty Treats* it is," said Ms. Colman. "I think that is a fine title. Thank you, class. Now, we are each going to draw some pictures for our cookbook. Draw items that you feel belong in a cookbook, such as vegetables, fruit, cooking utensils, and so on. The paper and markers are over here."

That was fun. I drew many different things: a mushroom, a banana, a chicken leg, a doughnut, a bowl of mashed potatoes. Later, we all turned in our drawings. Ms. Colman said she would use as many of them as possible in *Tasty Treats*.

I felt much better after I had turned in my drawings. Our cookbook was going to be very beautiful. And I was sure that I would hear from one of my celebrities soon.

Round Two

The next Saturday Nannie and I got up early. Nannie packed her car, the Pink Clinker, with all the things we would need for round two of the contest. Then she and I kissed our big-house family good-bye.

Round two was going to take place in Hartford, which is a pretty big city (and the capital of Connecticut). I have been there a bunch of times. On the way to Hartford we sang songs and played road games. Nannie is very good to travel with. In Hartford,

Nannie drove us right to the hotel where the contest would be held.

Inside, we were sent to a big ballroom, much bigger than the one at the hotel in Stoneybrook. There were rows and rows of tables with white cloths, just like last time.

Nannie gave her name to someone at the door, and he directed us to our table.

"Well, let's set up," said Nannie.

We put out our cookie sheets with waxed paper, and the bowl with the candle underneath to keep the chocolate warm. I started dipping pretzels and strawberries.

"Karen, look," whispered Nannie. "That man is a famous chef. And that man has his own restaurant here in Hartford."

"Gee," I said. Some of the contestants were even wearing tall white chef's hats.

"Oh, Karen, what am I doing here?" said Nannie. "I am a grandmother. I am not a professional cook. I wish we had not come today."

"Nannie!" I said in surprise. "You do not have to be a professional cook. Your Chocolate Magic will be the best thing those judges have ever tasted. I am sure of it. And being a grandmother is a very important job." I patted Nannie's hand. "Do not worry," I said. "You will do fine today. And I bet your Chocolate Magic will win a prize again. You will see."

Nannie smiled at me and gave me a hug. "Thank you, Karen," she said. "I feel better now. You are a great cheerleader."

I liked knowing that I had cheered up Nannie. "Look," I said. "I think the judges are getting started."

"And the first-place blue ribbon goes to . . . Janet Taylor!" said the head judge.

For a moment Nannie just stood there, her mouth open in surprise.

"Nannie! You won!" I cried. "Hooray!"

"Goodness! Why, I never expected this," said Nannie. She took the blue ribbon from the judge.

38

"Your Chocolate Magic is delicious," said the judge. "It is a perfect dipping chocolate. I am proud that it is made with Cocoa-Best chocolate."

"Why, thank you," said Nannie.

A reporter stuck a microphone under Nannie's nose. "What else is in it besides Cocoa-Best chocolate?"

Nannie drew herself up. "That is a secret," she said firmly. "My recipe is secret. I created it myself, with help from my granddaughter Karen Brewer."

I smiled for the camera.

"Have you thought about marketing your dipping chocolate?" asked the judge. He helped himself to another of our chocolate pretzels and took a bite.

"Oh, no," said Nannie, smiling. "I simply could not. I am very busy. I only entered the contest for fun."

"Maybe you should think about it," said the judge. "In the meantime, we expect to see you back here next week, for the third and final round of our contest."

"Yes, we will be here," said Nannie, putting her arm around me.

"Nannie's Chocolate Magic will win next week too!" I said.

"Maybe so, young lady," said the judge. "Maybe so."

None for Karen

"Yea!" cried Jannie Gilbert on Monday morning. "I have heard from my fifth celebrity!" She waved her letter around happily.

Boo and bullfrogs. Jannie, Pamela, Tammy, Sara, Ian, and Omar had heard from all five of their celebrities. Terri, Chris, Addie, Hank, Nancy, and Hannie had heard from four of their celebrities. Every single other person in my class had heard from at least three. Except for me. I had not heard from a single one.

"Maybe I forgot to put stamps on my letters," I said to Hannie and Nancy during recess.

"No." Nancy shook her head. "You did put stamps on them. I saw."

"Maybe all my celebrities are out of town," I said sadly.

"If they are, they are taking long vacations," said Hannie.

"Maybe my celebrities are all meaniemos," I said.

"You have just had bad luck," said Hannie. "It is weird that none of your celebrities have written back. But I bet it really is just bad luck. Maybe your letters came the same day they had to do a lot of other things, and they forgot about the recipes."

"Celebrities are very busy," Nancy pointed out.

"I know, but we will be sending the cookbook to be copied on Thursday," I said. "If I do not hear anything by then, I will not have a celebrity recipe in the cookbook."

"Try not to worry," said Nancy. "I am

sure that by Thursday you will have three recipes, at least."

"I am sure too," said Hannie.

I smiled at my two best friends. "Thanks."

But on Tuesday, nothing came for me. Hannie heard from her fifth celebrity. So did Nancy. So did Chris and Addie. Ricky, Natalie, and Leslie heard from their fourth celebrities. In two days we would take the cookbook to be copied. I would not have any recipes in it at all. I was the *only* one in my class who would not have anything. Double boo. Double bullfrogs.

Unless . . . Suddenly I had an idea.

The Secret Recipe

When I got home that day, Nannie was not there. She had taken Andrew to buy new sneakers. Kristy had fixed a snack for me, of apple slices and oatmeal cookies and a glass of milk.

"How is your class project going?" asked Kristy.

"Um, okay," I said. I took a bite of cookie.

"Have you heard from any of your celebrities yet?" she asked.

"No, not yet. But I have until tomorrow afternoon. And I have a backup plan."

45

"Oh, good," said Kristy. She took out a magazine and began to read.

I waited until Kristy went to her room to begin her homework. Then I raced to Nannie's recipe box. She keeps all of her recipes on index cards in a small wooden box that sits on our kitchen counter. I flipped through the dessert recipes until I found the one for Chocolate Magic. I tucked it under my shirt and ran upstairs to my room.

I closed my door quietly and sat at my desk. I took out a sheet of paper and began to copy the recipe for Chocolate Magic.

"One pound of chocolate," I wrote. I wanted to finish copying it before Nannie came home. Nannie would be so surprised to see her recipe for Chocolate Magic in our celebrity cookbook, I told myself. She would be the only person who was not a real celebrity. She would be very flattered, I decided. I did not listen to the voice in my head that reminded me that Nannie wanted to keep the recipe a secret. I was just too desperate.

I finished copying the recipe very fast. Then I snuck downstairs and put it back in Nannie's recipe box. There! Now I was all set.

"Ta-daa!" I said at school on Wednesday morning. I waved my paper around. "I have a recipe for our cookbook!"

"Good, Karen," said Ms. Colman. "But did you finally hear from one of your celebrities? The mail is not here yet."

"No," I said. "It is better than that. This is Nannie's amazing prizewinning recipe for dipping chocolate. She has been winning every contest she enters with this." For a moment I wondered if I should really hand in the recipe. Then I remembered that without Nannie's recipe I would have nothing in the cookbook.

I turned the recipe over to Addie. "Be very careful with this," I said. "This recipe is worth millions." I did not know if that was true. But it sounded good.

"Okay," said Addie. "I am glad you will

have a recipe, Karen. With this last one, we will have exactly eighty-five recipes. That is a lot."

"Our cookbook will have a hundred pages," said Ms. Colman. "That is a good size for a cookbook. And with all of your recipes and drawings in it, it will be very special. I think we will be able to sell a lot of copies, and make a lot of money for the library."

I smiled happily. I would not be the only one without a recipe in our book. Not anymore.

Karen's Clubhouse

That night Nannie made chicken and dumplings for dinner. I picked out all the dumplings and pushed them to one side of my plate. I do not like dumplings.

"How was everyone's day?" asked Elizabeth. "Andrew, you start."

"My day was fine," said Andrew. "It was my turn to hand out graham crackers at snack time. I was Miss Jewel's special helper." (Miss Jewel is Andrew's preschool teacher. He loves her.)

"I am sure you did a good job," said

Daddy. "Karen, how was your day?"

"Terrific," I said. "Tomorrow we will take our cookbook to be copied. It will be gigundoly wonderful."

"Will I be able to buy one?" asked Nannie.

"Um, well . . ." I said. I was not sure I wanted Nannie to see her recipe in our cookbook. But how could I keep her from seeing the book?

"On Friday we are unveiling our cookbook at the school library at one o'clock. We will have refreshments. If you want to buy a copy, you can come then."

"I will be first in line," said Nannie.

I tried to smile. I hoped maybe she would forget to come.

"My day stank," said David Michael. "I broke a shoelace. Lunch was yucky. And I lost my best marble during recess."

"I am sorry, honey," said Elizabeth. "I hope tomorrow is a better day for you."

"I had a not-so-great day," said Kristy. "At our Baby-sitters Club meeting we got only one phone call. I like it better when we are *too* busy than when we are not busy enough." (Kristy and a bunch of her friends run a baby-sitting service. They baby-sit for me, Andrew, Emily Michelle, David Michael, and lots of other kids.)

"I am sure it is a temporary lull," said Daddy. "Business will pick up soon."

"I hope so," said Kristy.

One by one the members of my big-house family talked about their days. It took awhile. One of the good things about the little house is that there are only four of us, so I stand out more. It is easy to get lost in all the action at the big house.

We had apple pie for dessert. Yum!

Daddy tapped his water glass. "Has everyone thought about the pantry? Remember, I asked for ideas about what to do with it."

"Yes!" said Kristy. "I have put a lot of thought into it. You know, it would be the perfect place for the Baby-sitters Club to meet — if I could have a phone line installed. I bet club dues would cover the cost of having another phone put in."

"Hmm," said Daddy. "I will consider it. Anyone else?"

"Yeah," said Sam. "If we wire the room for my stereo, then I could go in there and listen to music, and I would not disturb anyone. We could even soundproof the walls."

"Ah," said Daddy. "Next?"

"If you soundproof the walls, I could study in there," said Charlie. "Then I would not have to listen to everyone's racket all the time."

"Uh-huh," said Daddy.

"We could always use it for storage," said Elizabeth.

"Yes, that's true," said Daddy.

"If you turn it into a second playroom," said Andrew, "I would not have to go all the way upstairs to play. I could play down here too, and then I would be closer to the kitchen, for snacks."

"Good thinking," said Daddy.

Goody! It was my turn. I had been waiting for Daddy to ask us about the pantry. I had been thinking and thinking about it, and I had the perfect solution. "The Three Musketeers could use their own meeting place," I said. "You know, like Kristy's club. We could fix up the pantry and call it Karen's Clubhouse. Then the Three Musketeers could meet there all the time." I sat back, proud of my idea.

"I see," said Daddy. "Well, you have all given me ideas. I am not sure yet what I will do. But you have given me food for thought. Thank you."

"Daddy," I said. "When will you decide? I want to tell Hannie and Nancy about our clubhouse."

"Do not tell them anything yet," said Daddy. "I will try to decide within a few days."

I would just have to be patient. Boo.

11

The Not-So-Secret Recipe

On Thursday morning everyone in Ms. Colman's class got to see the final version of *Tasty Treats*. It looked terrific.

"See, there is an index, and a contents page," said Addie.

"There are different categories for the recipes," said Ricky.

"It looks so professional," I said. I was happy. Ms. Colman had chosen my drawing of a chicken leg to go in the Main Courses chapter. Not only that, but my mushroom drawing was in the Soups chapter, and my doughnut was in the Desserts chapter. She had chosen more of my drawings than anyone else's. It helped make up for my one recipe.

"I gave this chili recipe to my dad to make at home," said Chris. "It did not taste right."

"My mom made this carrot cake recipe," said Sara. "It was delicious."

"Well, some of the recipes will probably turn out a little better than others," said Ms. Colman. "We took out the really weird ones. I am pretty sure the ones that are left are okay."

"I wish one of our celebrities could see our cookbook," said Audrey.

"Here comes one now!" said Ms. Colman. "Hello, Mrs. Taylor. Welcome to our class."

I turned around and saw Nannie smiling at me. My stomach dropped. She held up my lunch. "You forgot this," she said.

"Oh, gee," I said. "I do not know how I forgot it. Thank you, Nannie." I swallowed hard.

"We were just looking at our cookbook,"

said Ms. Colman. "We feel it has come out very well. And I am glad to have the chance to thank you for your recipe."

Nannie raised her eyebrows. "My recipe?"

Oh, no, I thought.

"Yes," said Ms. Colman. "Your prize-winning recipe for Chocolate Magic. We were so pleased to include it in our cookbook." Ms. Colman turned the pages of the book and showed Nannie her recipe, in the Desserts chapter.

Nannie looked at the recipe, then at me. "My goodness," she said. She did not look at all flattered or proud. "Karen, will you walk me to the door, please?" she asked. Her voice was calm, but her eyes looked angry. "Good-bye, Ms. Colman."

At the door Nannie bent over to whisper to me. "Karen, I do not know what to say. I am very unhappy to see my recipe for Chocolate Magic in your school cookbook. I thought that recipe was our secret. I did not want to share it with anyone. And you did not even ask me if you could use it. I am so

surprised that I do not know what to think. But I am very upset."

"I am sorry, Nannie," I said. I had never seen Nannie so upset. "I thought you would not mind."

"You thought wrong," said Nannie. "We will discuss this further at home."

"I am sorry," I said again.

"I will see you later." Nannie turned and walked down the hall.

I slunk back to my seat. I had not meant to make Nannie angry. Now Ms. Colman was going to take the cookbook to the copier. We would make two hundred copies of Nannie's secret recipe. Nannie would probably be two hundred times as angry as she was now. What was I going to do?

Nannie Is Disappointed

All day long I felt bad about Nannie's recipe. I did not want to go home after school, but I had to.

When I am at the big house, I ride the school bus home with Hannie. (She lives across the street and one house down from the big house. Nancy lives next door to the little house.) On the way home, I told Hannie about my problem.

"All you can do is apologize," said Hannie. "She will understand."

I was not so sure.

Inside the big house a snack was waiting for me in the kitchen. Andrew and Kristy were already there.

"Where is Nannie?" I asked.

"I think she is in her room," said Kristy.

Upstairs, I knocked on Nannie's door. "May I come in?"

"Yes," said Nannie. She was sitting in her armchair by the window, sewing a button on one of Andrew's overalls.

"I came to apologize again," I said. "I feel terrible about the recipe. But none of my celebrities wrote back to me. I was the only one in my class who did not have a single celebrity recipe in the cookbook. So I took your Chocolate Magic recipe. I should have asked first. But I thought you would be happy to be the only person in our cookbook who was not exactly a celebrity."

"I would have been happy to lend you some other recipe," said Nannie. "If you had asked me, I would have helped you find a special one. But you took a recipe that

61

did not belong to you. A recipe I thought you knew was secret."

"Well, I am very sorry," I said. I could feel tears leaking into my eyes.

"I know that, Karen," said Nannie. She reached out and patted my shoulder. "But I still feel upset. And I think you need to learn not to take other people's things without asking. I think maybe I should go to the last round of the Cocoa-Best contest alone."

"But the contest is on Sunday! And I always go with you to help you!" I started to cry.

"I am sorry, Karen," said Nannie. "But I feel that maybe I should go alone. You were a big help at the first two contests, but now you have let me down."

I could not say anything. I turned and ran down the hall to my own room. I slammed the door shut and threw myself on my bed. Then I cried until dinnertime.

I could not eat much dinner. I was too miserable. Everyone knew what had happened, and they felt sorry for me. But they did not blame Nannie for not wanting me to go to the contest.

Nannie did not eat much either. She still looked upset.

After dinner I sat in my room and thought hard about how I could fix this problem. Crying had not solved anything (though it had made me feel a little better). I had done something wrong, and had made Nannie angry. Now what should I do?

Then I had an idea. I was not sure if it would work. But it was worth a try. I asked Elizabeth if I could use the phone to call Ms. Colman. She said yes.

"Ms. Colman?" I asked when she answered the phone. "This is Karen Brewer. I wanted to ask you — have you taken the cookbook to the copy center yet?"

"Yes, I have," said Ms. Colman. "I dropped it off this afternoon. Is there a problem?"

I told Ms. Colman everything — that I had taken the recipe without permission, and that Nannie was very upset.

"I am sorry, Karen," said Ms. Colman. "I know you have learned your lesson from this. But I cannot stop the copy center now — in fact, the cookbook has probably already been copied. I will try to think of a way to help you. I will see you tomorrow, all right?"

"All right," I said. I sighed. I would just have to wait. In the meantime, I told Nannie that I had tried to stop the copy center, but it was too late.

"Thank you for thinking of that," said Nannie. "It is too bad it did not work."

"Yes," I said unhappily. "Ms. Colman said she would try to help me tomorrow. Maybe she will have a good idea."

"I appreciate your trying to fix this problem," said Nannie. "I know you are very sorry."

I nodded. There was nothing else I could say.

Missing Page
Eighty-eight

On Friday morning I went to school still feeling sad. Nannie had forgiven me, but that did not make everything all right.

Today our cookbook would go on sale in the library.

I sat quietly on a bench until it was time to go inside. Hannie and Nancy sat quietly with me. (I had told Nancy all about my problem as soon as I had gotten to school.) That is because they are my best friends. If one of us feels sad, then we all feel sad. We are the Three Musketeers.

Soon we went into Ms. Colman's classroom.

"Karen, could you come here, please?" said Ms. Colman. She beckoned me to the front of her desk.

"I have been thinking about your problem," she said, very softly so no one else would hear. "I think I have a solution. It is not a perfect solution, but I think, for your grandmother's sake, we should do it."

"What is it?" I asked eagerly.

"All of them?" asked Hannie, wrinkling her nose.

"Yup," I said. "I better get started."

It was recess on Friday. Ms. Colman's solution had been for me to rip out one page of each cookbook — the page with Nannie's recipe on it. On the back of the page was only my drawing of a doughnut, so no other recipes would be lost. Then I had to go through all two hundred cookbooks and draw a black line through "Chocolate Magic" on the contents page in front, and in the index in back. It would be a big job. But it was the best thing to do.

"I will help you," said Nancy, pushing up her sleeves.

"Thank you very much," I said. "But I need to do this by myself, because it was my fault. If you want to stay here and talk to me, that would be a big help."

"Okay," said Nancy.

"I will stay too," said Hannie. "I do not need to go play outside."

I opened the first book and turned to page eighty-eight. It said, "Chocolate Magic, by Janet Taylor" on it. I ripped the page out. I took the next book and turned to page eighty-eight.

I did not finish during recess. Ms. Colman let me skip part of our art period so I could get all the books done.

In the end, I had a stack of two hundred page eighty-eights. I ripped them all in half and put them in the trash. I sighed. Now I

had absolutely *no* recipes in the cookbook, and only two drawings. I was the only person in my class with no recipes.

I wanted to tell Nannie about Ms. Colman's solution. But I would have to wait until I got home after school. I hoped Nannie would feel less upset.

In the meantime our class had to get ready for the cookbook publishing party in the library.

14

Buy Your *Tasty Treats* Here!

As soon as I finished with the cookbooks, our school custodian Mr. Thompson helped us carry them to the library. We set up a large poster that said:

Buy your *Tasty Treats* cookbook here.
Only $10.
All proceeds to go to the library fund.

(Proceeds means money.)

Ms. Colman had set up a long table with a paper tablecloth on it. It reminded me of all the contest tables I had seen with Nannie, and I felt sad again. But I could not sit around feeling sad. There was work to do.

On one end of the table we stacked up some cookbooks.

On the other end we put trays of refreshments. All the refreshments had been made using *Tasty Treats* recipes. (I had not made anything. You know why.)

Addie had made Mexican wedding cookies. Her favorite singer, Serena Lopez, had sent the recipe. Chris Lamar had made Tough Tommy Blackcat's bean dip. (I hoped Bobby would not sing that song again.) There were also cupcakes, chicken wings, punch, and a macaroni salad.

Because I had not contributed any food, my job was to set up the paper plates and napkins. I tried to arrange them neatly. Sara Ford stacked paper cups at one end. Ian put plastic forks in a pile.

When everything was ready our librarian

opened the door of the library. We had invited the other second-graders, Mr. Berger's class, to join us. Many kids had also invited family members.

"Hi, Mommy!" said Nancy. Mrs. Dawes saw her and waved.

"Hello, Karen," said a voice. I turned around.

"Daddy!" I said. "I did not expect to see you here."

"Nannie asked me to come buy her a *Tasty Treats* cookbook," said Daddy. "She is busy getting ready for the contest on Sunday. But she would like to have a copy of the book you worked so hard on."

"They are right over here," I said, pointing. "But you will see it is missing page eighty-eight. They all are. I took out all the page eighty-eights so that Nannie's recipe would not be in the books."

"I am sure Nannie will be very glad to hear that," said Daddy. He gave Ms. Colman the money and picked up a copy of *Tasty Treats*. He opened it and flipped through the pages. "This looks very nice, Karen," he said. "Your class did a super job."

"Thank you," I said. "I do not have any recipes in it, but that is my drawing of a chicken leg on page thirty-two. And there is my drawing of a mushroom."

Daddy found the drawings. "They are excellent, Karen. They look almost good enough to eat."

I giggled. I felt better. Nannie had wanted a cookbook anyway. I had gotten to see Daddy in the middle of the day. And Nannie's prizewinning recipe was still a secret.

The Pantry

"Hello, hello, hello!" I called. "I am home!"

I ran into the big-house kitchen. I was hoping Nannie would be there, waiting for me with a snack. Andrew and Kristy were there. So was Sam. They were all eating peanut-butter crackers.

"Where is Nannie?" I asked. "I have something important to tell her."

"She went to the fancy baking shop downtown," said Kristy. "She wanted to get some special foil papers to use for her chocolates at the contest on Sunday."

"Oh." My good mood turned a tiny bit blue. I was thinking about the contest on Sunday — the one Nannie wanted me to stay home from.

Bam! Bam! Bam! The sudden loud noise made me jump.

"What is that?" I asked.

Just then a workman came through the kitchen. His clothes were dusty. He was wearing a mask over part of his face. He pushed it down and smiled at me.

"Hello," he said. "Just passing through."

"Hello," I said.

"Watson has hired some people to work on the pantry," Kristy explained. (Watson is what Elizabeth's kids call Daddy.)

Hooray! "Are they turning it into Karen's Clubhouse?"

"No." Kristy laughed. "Watson has not decided what it will be yet. But he wanted to start clearing it out and fixing it up."

I took a peanut-butter cracker and went to the pantry to see what was going on.

Daddy was standing in the doorway.

"Yes, we should get rid of that sink. I will replace it," he was saying.

From inside the pantry I could hear pounding and scraping noises, and other voices.

"Hi, Daddy," I said. "What are you doing?"

"I am figuring out how to fix up the pantry," he said. "We have cleared out all the old junk that no one uses. Now the workmen are repairing the walls and the window. They will also put in a new sink and perhaps some cupboards."

I peered in through the open door. The pantry was all dirty and dusty. Two men were scraping paint off a wall by the window.

"It would be a great clubhouse," I said.

Daddy scratched his chin. "It would be good for a lot of different things," he said. "For example, I could keep all of my fishing equipment in here."

"Oh," I said.

"But I have not decided yet," said Daddy. "I am still open to ideas."

"Okay. Thank you for coming to school today. It cheered me up," I said.

"You are welcome," said Daddy. He turned to talk to the workmen. I headed back to the kitchen to finish my snack.

The pantry would be the coolest clubhouse, I thought. But the Three Musketeers are not really a club. And we could always get together in my bedroom, or at Hannie's house or Nancy's house. I decided I would not be heartbroken if Daddy did not let me have the pantry as a clubhouse.

In the meantime there was something I wanted to do for Nannie before she got home.

16

Good Luck, Nannie

I still wished Nannie would take me to the final round of her contest. But I understood why she did not want to. I had let her down.

But even if I could not go, I wanted Nannie to win. At school I had tried to think of ways I could make up with Nannie. I decided that it would be nice to make her a good-luck charm to take to the contest. That way she would know that I was still thinking of her, even though I was not with her.

I sat at my desk and pulled out my art

supplies. A pin would be a good idea, I thought. Then Nannie could wear it.

I found my modeling clay that hardens when you bake it. I shaped it into a smiling mouth. I made little teeth inside. Then I stuck a large safety pin to the back.

I asked Kristy to bake it for me in the toaster oven. She did. (I am not allowed to use the toaster oven by myself.) It baked in just twenty minutes. Then it had to cool off for awhile.

I painted the lips red and the teeth white. It looked like a nice big happy smile. I hoped Nannie would like it.

After dinner I found Nannie in the play-room. She was getting ready to play Candy-land with Andrew and Emily Michelle.

"May I talk to you for a minute, Nannie?" I asked politely. "It will not take long."

"Certainly," said Nannie. "I will be right back, Andrew."

We went down the hall to my room.

"First, I want to tell you about Ms. Colman's solution," I said. "I do not know if you have looked at your copy of *Tasty Treats* yet. But today, before the cookbooks went on sale, I ripped out all the page eighty-eights and threw them away. Then I scratched 'Chocolate Magic' out of the contents and the index. In every single book."

"Really?" said Nannie. She looked surprised. "Wasn't there another recipe on the other side of page eighty-eight?"

"No. It was just my drawing of a doughnut," I said. "So it was okay. Even though now there are no page eighty-eights. But at least no one will see your secret chocolate recipe."

"Goodness," said Nannie. "It sounds as if you went to a lot of trouble. And it means that your doughnut drawing will not be in the cookbooks."

"That is okay," I said. I took out my smiling-mouth pin. "Here. I made this good-luck pin for you to wear at the contest on Sunday. The smiling mouth is to remind you of me. And it also shows what someone will do as soon as they taste Chocolate Magic." I gave it to Nannie, and she pinned it on her sweater.

"It is lovely, Karen," said Nannie. "It is very cheerful, and I am glad you made it for me. I am also glad that you and Ms. Colman fixed the cookbooks. Thank you."

"You are welcome," I said. "I will never do anything like that again."

Nannie laughed and hugged me close. "I am sure you will do something different next time," she said.

I laughed too.

"Karen, I have been thinking," said Nannie. "You have been very grown-up and taken care of the recipe problem all by yourself. And I feel that I just will not do well at the contest without you. Even with your good-luck pin. I think maybe *you* are my good-luck charm. Will you come to the contest on Sunday and help me, like you did with the last two?"

81

I started jumping up and down. "Yes! Yes, Nannie! I would love to."

"Good. It is all settled, then," said Nannie. "Now I better go play Candyland with Andrew and Emily Michelle."

"I will play too," I said.

The Final Round

"There it is!" I said, pointing out the window.

Daddy turned the minivan into the parking lot of the hotel. We were at the big hotel in Hartford again. But this was the last, and most important, part of the contest.

Because it was so important, my whole big-house family had decided to come. In Daddy's minivan were Daddy, Charlie, Sam, David Michael, me, and Andrew. In Nannie's Pink Clinker were Nannie, Elizabeth, Kristy, and Emily Michelle.

Inside the hotel we helped Nannie get ready. While Nannie filled in the contest forms, I showed everyone where we needed to go. I had done this already. I was an expert.

"This is our table," I said briskly. "Sam, you set up the bowl and the candle. Kristy, please help me unload our samples. Andrew, will you set up our sign, please?"

By the time Nannie had registered, her table was all ready.

"Thank you, everyone," she said. "It looks perfect." She got busy melting some Chocolate Magic. I handed her some fruit, some pretzels, and some tiny cake squares to dip. Elizabeth got a cookie sheet ready with some waxed paper on it.

"I have something too," said Daddy. He opened a shopping bag and pulled out ten baseball caps. They were pink. On each hat was written TEAM NANNIE in black thread.

"Oh, Watson, thank you," Nannie said, laughing.

We each put on a hat. I loved mine. It

showed that we were a family, and we were all working together.

This contest was much bigger than either of the first two Nannie had competed in. The hotel ballroom was crowded with rows of tables. There were separate sections for "Baked Goods," "Candies," and "Sauces and Dips." Ten people were in our section!

Many people had bought tickets to watch the judging. (They would get to eat the samples afterward.)

There were five judges this time, three men and two women. Slowly they worked their way around the room, tasting and testing each entry. Between each sample they sipped water. Sometimes they ate a cracker. Daddy said this was to clear the chocolate from their mouths so that they could really taste the next sample.

The judges stepped up to Nannie's table. They saw my glittery CHOCOLATE MAGIC sign and smiled. One by one they each tasted Nannie's samples. First a strawberry, then a pretzel. Two judges tried the little cakes.

I was practically quivering with excitement. I wanted to jump up and scream, "Well?" Instead I just crossed my fingers.

The judges made notes in their notebooks. They whispered to each other. Then they smiled at Nannie and moved on to the next table. The man next to us was also competing with a dipping chocolate. His samples sat in tiny gold foil wrappers. His business cards were in a holder on his table. He was a pro.

All we could do now was wait. I ate a chocolate-dipped pretzel to help me calm down. After about twenty minutes, the judges headed for the stage at one end of the ballroom. They huddled together near the microphone, talking and comparing notes.

"This is driving me crazy," said Sam, sitting on a cardboard box.

"I cannot stand the tension," Kristy agreed. "I cannot believe so many people entered this contest."

"These are earlier contest winners from all

over the Northeast," Nannie pointed out. "They are from many different cities and states."

"Do not worry, Mom," said Elizabeth. "Your Chocolate Magic is the very best."

"Ahem," said a judge, tapping the microphone. "After a great deal of thought, we have decided on a winner!"

18

And the Winner Is . . .

"Thank you all for coming today," said the judge. "We were most impressed with the quality of the entries, and the many delicious treats we tasted. As you know, there will be one first-place prize, one second-place prize, and one third-place prize given in each category. And then there will be one grand prize awarded to the recipe that uses Cocoa-Best chocolate in the best way."

"Cut to the chase," muttered Charlie. "Just tell us who won."

"Starting with the third-place prize in the

'Baked Goods' category . . ." said the judge.

We all groaned.

Nannie did not win the third-place prize in the "Sauces and Dips" category. She did not win the second-place prize. We all held our breath when they announced the first-place winner.

"And the blue ribbon goes to . . . Alex McCall!" said the judge.

The man next to us smiled and trotted to the stage to receive his award.

Nannie's shoulders slumped. She did not look at any of us. We were all very surprised and very, very disappointed. After all of Nannie's hard work, she had not won. Even after I had made her that great sign with glitter. And I had helped her choose perfect strawberries. We had used only the best pretzels. I had been so sure she would win.

"And the grand-prize winner of the Cocoa-Best Chocolate Cook-off is . . ." said the judge.

Nannie started to gather her things together for the long car ride home.

"Janet Taylor, of Stoneybrook, Connecticut, with her Chocolate Magic dipping chocolate recipe!" said the judge.

Nannie dropped a tray of samples and stared at the stage.

"Nannie!" I yelled. "You did it! You did it again!"

"Mom, you won!" said Elizabeth. She grabbed Nannie and hugged her. Then we all began to jump up and down and shout. Daddy threw his "Team Nannie" cap in the air. Kristy and Sam hit high fives. Even David Michael and I hugged each other. (We do not do that very often.)

"Oh, my goodness," said Nannie. "My goodness."

A swarm of people crowded our table. The judges handed Nannie a gigundo trophy. It was a marble pillar with a large golden bar of Cocoa-Best chocolate on top.

"Congratulations, Mrs. Taylor," said the main judge. "Your dipping chocolate is the best I have ever tasted. You really should think about selling it."

"Hmm," said Nannie. She had a huge smile on her face.

"Along with this beautiful Cocoa-Best trophy," said another judge, "is this check for three thousand dollars."

"Good heavens," said Nannie.

"Plus, here is a gift certificate for two hundred dollars' worth of Cocoa-Best chocolate," said a third judge.

"Oh, lovely," said Nannie.

"And last but not least, here is a gift certificate for you and your entire family to have dinner at the restaurant of your choice."

Nannie laughed and waved her hand at all of us. "I do not think you knew there were ten people in my family," she said.

We smiled at the judges. They smiled back.

"That does not matter, Mrs. Taylor," said a judge. "Dinner is on us."

Guess where we went to dinner. Chez Maurice. It is the fanciest restaurant in all of

Stoneybrook. My whole family put on party clothes. I wore a blue velvet dress, with white tights and shiny black shoes.

At the restaurant, I tapped my water glass with my spoon.

"Ahem," I said. "I would like to make a toast. Here's to Nannie, who has won the biggest contest I have ever seen, with her super-special *and* super-secret recipe for Chocolate Magic!"

The people in my family raised their glasses.

"Hear, hear," said Daddy.

"Thank you very much," said Nannie. "And extra thanks to my special assistant, Karen. I could not have done it without her help."

I smiled. It had been a wonderful day.

Chocolate Magic, Inc.

"Class," said Ms. Colman on Monday, "I am pleased to tell you that our *Tasty Treats* cookbook is selling very nicely."

"Yippee!" I shouted.

"Karen, indoor voice, please," said Ms. Colman.

"Sorry," I whispered.

"In fact, it is such a big success that we are thinking about printing more of them."

"All right!" said Bobby.

"Cool!" said Addie.

"And I would like to ask Karen to ask

Nannie if she would like to contribute one nonsecret recipe to the second edition of our cookbook. We will make a new page eighty-eight with her recipe."

I smiled. "That is a great idea," I said. "I will ask her tonight." This was wonderful news. I might have a recipe in our cookbook after all!

That night at dinner I asked Nannie for a recipe. She said she would be happy to give me one.

"Now I have an announcement to make," said Nannie. "I have been thinking a great deal about Chocolate Magic. I had a lot of fun entering the contest. I found I really enjoyed the challenge. While I will always see my main job as taking care of this family, I have decided that I will have another job too. I am planning on going into business for myself."

"Really?" said Elizabeth. "What are you going to do?"

Suddenly I felt worried. Daddy would be

busy working in his home office. Elizabeth worked at her office. If Nannie worked too, who would I talk to when I got home from school? Who would help me with my homework, and do things with me in the afternoon? And what about Andrew and Emily Michelle? They are just little kids. They need Nannie too.

"I am planning to sell Chocolate Magic," said Nannie. "That is something I can do part-time, from home. I could use Chocolate Magic in all kinds of ways — in centerpieces for tables, in gift baskets, for special holiday desserts. I love making gift baskets and centerpieces. I could do all sorts of things with it."

"Gee," said Elizabeth. "That sounds like a wonderful idea."

"If I set up my business here at home, I can still take care of the kids, and also help around the house, the way I do now," said Nannie.

I felt much better.

"But having my own business would be

97

fun and exciting for me," said Nannie.

"It sounds like a terrific idea," said Daddy. "In fact, it would be selfish of you to keep Chocolate Magic from the rest of the world."

We all laughed.

"And I have a good idea," said Daddy. "You will need a special place for your business. A place here in the house where you will have plenty of space and will not be disturbed. I would like you to have the renovated pantry for your business."

"Oh, Watson," said Nannie. "That is a wonderful idea. But are you sure you do not need the room for anything else?"

"No," said Daddy. "Your Chocolate Magic business is the best use I have heard for the pantry. It is yours. You will need to tell the workmen what to do with the room so that you have a good work space."

"Thank you very much, Watson," said Nannie. "The pantry will be perfect."

"What can I do to help, Nannie?" asked

Kristy. "Maybe I can hand out your business cards to our baby-sitting clients."

"I can tell people at school," said Charlie.

"Watson and I can mention it to people we work with," said Elizabeth.

Nannie smiled at us. "What a wonderful family I have," she said. "Thank you all. I know I will need lots of help."

"You can count on us, Nannie," I said.

She patted my hand. "I know."

20

Out With the Old, In With the New

"Watch out," said Sam. "Ladder coming through."

It was the very next weekend. We were all crowded into the pantry, helping Nannie turn it into a good workplace. Daddy had had a phone installed. There were new shelves on the walls, and new cabinets with countertops. The window had been repaired so it would not leak when it rained.

Nannie would still have to prepare and

cook Chocolate Magic in the kitchen. But once it was made, she could do everything else in this pantry: take orders, make baskets, create special decorations. She had used her prize money to buy many of the supplies she would need, such as white cardboard boxes to package her chocolates in, woven baskets, and ribbons in all colors.

Daddy was on a ladder now, hanging a new light fixture from the ceiling. Elizabeth and Kristy were on step stools. They were lining the new shelves with flowered paper. Sam and Charlie were putting the handles on the cabinet doors.

Emily Michelle was sitting on the floor, playing with her own small kitchen set.

Andrew was sorting all the boxes and tissue paper and ribbons that Nannie would use.

I had a very special job: I was painting a mural on one wall. The mural showed Nannie in her "Kiss the Cook" apron. She was wearing a "Team Nannie" baseball cap. In one hand she held a wire whisk to stir with.

In the other hand was a bar of Cocoa-Best chocolate. I painted a smile on her face. Also in the picture I painted her big Cocoa-Best trophy, and a large blue first-place ribbon.

"That is lovely, Karen," said Nannie. "That picture makes me feel like a winner — as if I can do anything."

That made me feel very good inside.

Soon Nannie's pantry was all ready. Nannie had even gotten business cards. They said:

Janet Taylor's
Chocolate Magic —
Gifts for all occasions

The big-house address and her phone number were printed on the back.

Now we had to wait for Nannie's first order.

"Well, Mom, what are you doing tomorrow?" asked Elizabeth a few days later.

"I am going to take Emily Michelle to get

a haircut," said Nannie. "And I will probably go to the grocery store. Why?"

"Because you might have to stay home and make . . . Chocolate Magic!" said Elizabeth. She waved a piece of paper in the air. "This is an order from Beth Cooper, at my office. She is throwing a baby shower for her sister this weekend. She is looking for special gift baskets to place on each table at the luncheon. I told her about Chocolate Magic, and she said it sounds perfect."

"Hooray, Nannie!" I said. "Your first order!" I felt very excited for Nannie. After all, I had helped her come up with the recipe in the first place. We were practically in business together.

"I will be happy to create something for her," said Nannie. "Ask her to call me so we can discuss all the details."

"Okay," said Elizabeth. "Congratulations, Mom."

"Thank you. I will need just one thing before I make the gift baskets for Ms. Cooper," said Nannie.

"What is that?" asked Elizabeth.

"My special helper, of course," said Nannie, turning to me. "Karen, what are *you* doing tomorrow?"

I jumped up and grabbed my "Team Nannie" cap.

"I am going to go to school," I said. "And then I will rush home to make some Chocolate Magic!"

Nannie gave me a big hug. "Together, Karen, we can do anything!"

"You are so right," I said.

L. GODWIN

About the Author

ANN M. MARTIN lives in New York City and loves animals, especially cats. She has two cats of her own, Gussie and Woody.

Other books by Ann M. Martin that you might enjoy are *Stage Fright*; *Me and Katie (the Pest)*; and the books in *The Baby-sitters Club* series.

Ann likes ice cream and *I Love Lucy*. And she has her own little sister, whose name is Jane.

Little Sister

Don't Miss #94

KAREN'S SNOW PRINCESS

I read the flyer from start to finish. It said the winners would get to ride a parade float.

Being Snow Princess sounded very cool. I am good at writing essays and compositions. And I am good at giving speeches too. So I probably had a good chance of winning the contest if I entered. But there was one big problem. I had my heart set on lighting up the town square. If I were Snow Princess, I was sure the mayor would not pick me. After all, she could not let one person do *everything*. Even if that one person was me, Karen Brewer.

LITTLE APPLE™

Little Sister

by Ann M. Martin,
author of The Baby-sitters Club ®

☐	MQ44300-3	#1	Karen's Witch	$2.95
☐	MQ44258-9	#5	Karen's School Picture	$2.95
☐	MQ43651-1	#10	Karen's Grandmothers	$2.95
☐	MQ43645-7	#15	Karen's In Love	$2.95
☐	MQ44823-4	#20	Karen's Carnival	$2.95
☐	MQ44831-5	#25	Karen's Pen Pal	$2.95
☐	MQ45645-8	#30	Karen's Kittens	$2.95
☐	MQ45652-0	#35	Karen's Doll Hospital	$2.95
☐	MQ47040-X	#40	Karen's Newspaper	$2.95
☐	MQ47044-2	#45	Karen's Twin	$2.95
☐	MQ47048-5	#50	Karen's Lucky Penny	$2.95
☐	MQ48230-0	#55	Karen's Magician	$2.95
☐	MQ48305-6	#60	Karen's Pony	$2.95
☐	MQ25998-9	#65	Karen's Toys	$2.95
☐	MQ26280-7	#70	Karen's Grandad	$2.95
☐	MQ69183-X	#75	Karen's County Fair	$2.95
☐	MQ69188-0	#80	Karen's Christmas Tree	$2.99
☐	MQ69193-7	#85	Karen's Treasure	$2.99
☐	MQ69194-5	#86	Karen's Telephone Trouble	$3.50
☐	MQ06585-8	#87	Karen's Pony Camp	$3.50
☐	MQ06586-6	#88	Karen's Puppet Show	$3.50
☐	MQ06587-4	#89	Karen's Unicorn	$3.50
☐	MQ06588-2	#90	Karen's Haunted House	$3.50
☐	MQ06589-0	#91	Karen's Pilgrim	$3.50
☐	MQ55407-7	BSLS Jump Rope Rhymes		$5.99
☐	MQ73914-X	BSLS Playground Games		$5.99
☐	MQ89735-7	BSLS Photo Scrapbook Book and Camera Package		$9.99

Available wherever you buy books, or use this order form.

Scholastic Inc., P.O. Box 7502, 2931 E. McCarty Street, Jefferson City, MO 65102

Please send me the books I have checked above. I am enclosing $ _____
(please add $2.00 to cover shipping and handling). Send check or money order – no
cash or C.O.Ds please.

Name _____ Birthdate _____

Address _____

City _____ State/Zip _____

Please allow four to six weeks for delivery. Offer good in U.S.A. only. Sorry, mail orders are not
available to residents to Canada. Prices subject to change.

BLSG497